'Arry & Bert

Based on *The Railway Series* by the Rev. W. Awdry

Illustrations by
Robin Davies and Jerry Smith

EGMONT

EGMONT

We bring stories to life

First published in Great Britain in 2006
by Egmont UK Limited
239 Kensington High Street, London W8 6SA
All Rights Reserved

Thomas the Tank Engine & Friends™

A BRITT ALLCROFT COMPANY PRODUCTION

Based on The Railway Series by The Reverend W Awdry
© 2007 Gullane (Thomas) LLC. A HIT Entertainment Company

Thomas the Tank Engine & Friends and Thomas & Friends are trademarks of Gullane (Thomas) Limited.
Thomas the Tank Engine & Friends and Design is Reg. US. Pat. & Tm. Off.

HiT entertainment

ISBN 978 1 4052 2363 8
5 7 9 10 8 6 4
Printed in Great Britain

The Forest Stewardship Council (FSC) is an international, non-governmental organisation
dedicated to promoting responsible management of the world's forests. FSC operates a
system of forest certification and product labelling that allows consumers to identify
wood and wood-based products from well managed forests.

For more information about Egmont's paper buying policy please visit www.egmont.co.uk/ethicalpublishing

For more information about the FSC please visit their website at www.fsc.uk.org

This is a story about 'Arry and Bert the Diesels. They liked playing tricks on the steam engines and getting them into trouble. But one Halloween, their trick backfired ...

It was Halloween on the Island of Sodor! The engines were enjoying picking up passengers dressed as monsters, witches and wizards.

Thomas and Emily were going on a night run that evening. They were collecting iron trucks from 'Arry and Bert at the Smelter's yard, which had to be delivered to the Harbour before sunrise.

Percy thought Halloween was scary, so he was glad that he had not been chosen for the job.

At the end of the day, the tired engines returned to Tidmouth sheds. It was now time for Thomas and Emily to go on their night run.

"Be careful at the Smelter's yard," Percy warned. "It can be rather dark and creepy there after dark."

"There's nothing to be afraid of," said Thomas, confidently. "There's no such thing as ghosts."

"Ghosts are just silly make believe," Emily added, as they steamed away.

Thomas and Emily raced across the Island. They liked travelling at night, passing owls and foxes as they went.

"Peep! Peep! It seems quieter than ever tonight," Thomas said to Emily.

"It's very dark, too," Emily said, a little timidly.

By the time they reached the Smelter's yard, Emily felt a little nervous. She looked for 'Arry and Bert, but couldn't see them anywhere. She thought they must be in the Smelter's shed so she made her way towards it with Thomas following behind.

"There's no need to worry," Thomas said, as he and Emily moved through the dark yard.
But then they heard a huge crash!

"What was that?" Emily shouted, fearfully.

"The wind must have knocked something over," Thomas replied, but he didn't believe that was true. His pistons rattled as he trembled. He didn't feel so brave any more.

Hiding in the shadows, 'Arry and Bert smiled. Bert pushed an oil drum, causing it to crash to the ground.

Thomas and Emily jumped as they heard it. And as they passed the hiding diesels, 'Arry and Bert moaned and groaned, like scary ghosts.

"Cinders and ashes!" Thomas said, in surprise.

"This place is haunted!" cried Emily, as she rushed towards the shed. She wanted to fetch the trucks and leave the scary place as soon as possible.

In the shed, Emily saw the trucks they had come to collect. She moved towards them without noticing a white sheet hanging from the ceiling above her. As she passed underneath, it caught on her fender and suddenly fell on her.

"Aarrgh!" she cried. "A ghost has got me!" She raced to the door, trying to get away from it.

When Thomas saw what looked like a ghost engine coming towards him, he forgot about the iron trucks and ran away. Emily, covered by the sheet, raced after him.

'Arry and Bert were waiting outside. They were looking forward to laughing at Thomas and Emily for being such scaredy engines. But when they saw Thomas being chased by a ghost engine, they were scared, too!

"Oh, no! There really is a ghost!" cried 'Arry.

"Let's get out of here!" shouted Bert and they turned and fled.

'Arry, Bert and Thomas raced across the Island, followed by the 'ghost engine'. As they neared Tidmouth sheds, Thomas frantically whistled to wake the other engines.

Yawning loudly, Percy said, "Whatever is the matter Thomas?"

"There's a ghost engine after us!" cried Thomas. "Look! Here it comes!"

Everyone gasped when they saw it approaching. They couldn't believe their eyes.

But as the 'ghost' went under a signal, the corner of the sheet caught on it, and as Emily rushed forward, the sheet fell to the ground behind her.

"It looks like Emily is your ghost!" giggled Percy, as the other engines all laughed.

'Arry, Bert and Thomas felt very foolish. Emily was just relieved that there was no ghost, after all.

The Fat Controller came to the shed to find out what was happening. Thomas told him about the spooky noises that had made him and Emily think the Smelter's yard was haunted.

"So when the sheet fell on me, I thought it really was a ghost!" Emily said, with a smile.

"Do you know anything about this?" The Fat Controller asked 'Arry and Bert, who meekly nodded. "In that case," he said, "*you* will deliver the trucks to the Harbour tonight and while you're doing that, you can think about all the trouble your trick has caused!"

'**A**rry and Bert apologised to The Fat Controller and set off to the Smelter's yard to fetch the trucks. As they disappeared into the distance, the steam engines heard them arguing about whose idea it had been.

"Now we've established that there *are* no ghosts, we can all go back to sleep!" The Fat Controller said to the other engines.

The engines were relieved that there were no ghosts, but they all agreed it would be a long time before they forgot the sight of Emily the 'ghost' engine!

The Thomas Story Library is THE definitive collection of stories about Thomas and ALL his friends.

There are now 50 stories
from the Island of Sodor
to collect!

So go on, start your Thomas Story Library NOW!

A Fantastic Offer for Thomas the Tank Engine Fans!

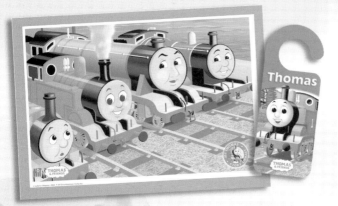

STICK POUND COIN HERE

In every Thomas Story Library book like this one, you will find a special token. Collect 6 Thomas tokens and we will send you a brilliant Thomas poster, and a double-sided bedroom door hanger! Simply tape a £1 coin in the space above, and fill out the form overleaf.

Cut along the dotted line

TO BE COMPLETED BY AN ADULT

To apply for this great offer, ask an adult to complete the coupon below and send it with a pound coin and 6 tokens, to:
THOMAS OFFERS, PO BOX 715, HORSHAM RH12 5WG

☐ Please send a Thomas poster and door hanger. I enclose 6 tokens plus a £1 coin. (Price includes P&P)

Fan's name...

Address..

....Postcode...............................

Date of birth...

Name of parent/guardian...

Signature of parent/guardian..

Please allow 28 days for delivery. Offer is only available while stocks last. We reserve the right to change the terms of this offer at any time and we offer a 14 day money back guarantee. This does not affect your statutory rights.

☐ Data Protection Act: If you do not wish to receive other similar offers from us or companies we recommend, please tick this box. Offers apply to UK only.

Cut along the dotted line